GAULISH VILLAGE

COMPENDIUM

LAUDANUM

AQUARIUM

TOTORUM

ARMORICA

BELGICA

LUTETIA

SPQR

GAUL
(ROMAN CONQUEST)
50 BC

CELTICA

AQUITANIA

PROVINCIA

THE YEAR IS 50 BC. GAUL IS ENTIRELY OCCUPIED BY THE
ROMANS. WELL, NOT ENTIRELY ... ONE SMALL VILLAGE OF
INDOMITABLE GAULS STILL HOLDS OUT AGAINST THE INVADERS.
AND LIFE IS NOT EASY FOR THE ROMAN LEGIONARIES WHO
GARRISON THE FORTIFIED CAMPS OF TOTORUM, AQUARIUM,
LAUDANUM AND COMPENDIUM ...

ASTERIX, THE HERO OF THESE ADVENTURES. A SHREWD, CUNNING LITTLE WARRIOR, ALL PERILOUS MISSIONS ARE IMMEDIATELY ENTRUSTED TO HIM. ASTERIX GETS HIS SUPERHUMAN STRENGTH FROM THE MAGIC POTION BREWED BY THE DRUID GETAFIX . . .

OBELIX, ASTERIX'S INSEPARABLE FRIEND. A MENHIR DELIVERY MAN BY TRADE, ADDICTED TO WILD BOAR, OBELIX IS ALWAYS READY TO DROP EVERYTHING AND GO OFF ON A NEW ADVENTURE WITH ASTERIX – SO LONG AS THERE'S WILD BOAR TO EAT, AND PLENTY OF FIGHTING. HIS CONSTANT COMPANION IS DOGMATIX, THE ONLY KNOWN CANINE ECOLOGIST, WHO HOWLS WITH DESPAIR WHEN A TREE IS CUT DOWN.

GETAFIX, THE VENERABLE VILLAGE DRUID, GATHERS MISTLETOE AND BREWS MAGIC POTIONS. HIS SPECIALITY IS THE POTION WHICH GIVES THE DRINKER SUPERHUMAN STRENGTH. BUT GETAFIX ALSO HAS OTHER RECIPES UP HIS SLEEVE . . .

CACOFONIX, THE BARD. OPINION IS DIVIDED AS TO HIS MUSICAL GIFTS. CACOFONIX THINKS HE'S A GENIUS. EVERY-ONE ELSE THINKS HE'S UNSPEAKABLE. BUT AS LONG AS HE DOESN'T SPEAK, LET ALONE SING, EVERYBODY LIKES HIM . . .

FINALLY, VITALSTATISTIX, THE CHIEF OF THE TRIBE. MAJESTIC, BRAVE AND HOT-TEMPERED, THE OLD WARRIOR IS RESPECTED BY HIS MEN AND FEARED BY HIS ENEMIES. VITALSTATISTIX HIMSELF HAS ONLY ONE FEAR, HE IS AFRAID THAT THE SKY MAY FALL ON HIS HEAD TOMORROW. BUT AS HE ALWAYS SAYS, TOMORROW NEVER COMES.

GOSCINNY AND UD
PRESENT

An Aster

ASTERIX CHIEF DAUG

Written by JEʎ
Illustrated by D
Translated by AL

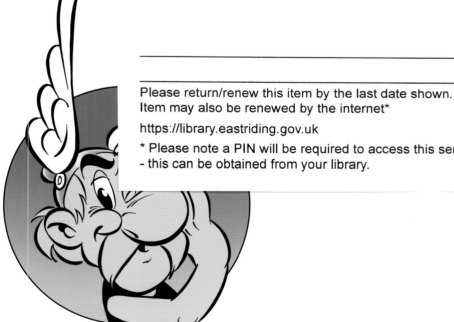

Colour by Thierry Mébarki

Orion

www.asterix.com   f Asterix and Obelix   @lartdasterix

With heartfelt thanks to Anthea Bell for her wonderful translation work on ASTERIX over the years.
Les Éditions Albert René and Orion Children's Books

Asterix titles available now

ORION CHILDREN'S BOOKS

First published in Great Britain in 2019 by Hodder & Stoughton

1 3 5 7 9 10 8 6 4 2

ASTERIX®-OBELIX®-IDEFIX®-DOGMATIX®
Original edition © 2019 Les Éditions Albert René
English translation © 2019 Les Éditions Albert René
Original title: *La Fille de Vercingétorix*
Exclusive licensee: Hachette Children's Group
Translator: Adriana Hunter
Typography: Arvind Shah

The right of Jean-Yves Ferri to be identified as the author of this work and
the right of Didier Conrad to be identified as the illustrator of this work have been
asserted by them in accordance with the Copyright, Designs and Patents Act 1988.

A CIP catalogue record for this book is available from the British Library.

ISBN 978-1-5101-0713-7 (hardback)
ISBN 978-1-5101-0714-4 (paperback)
ISBN 978-1-5101-0720-5 (ebook)

Printed and bound in Italy by Printer Trento S.R.L
The paper and board used in this book are from well-managed forests and other responsible sources.

Orion Children's Books
An imprint of Hachette Children's Group
Part of Hodder & Stoughton
Carmelite House, 50 Victoria Embankment
London EC4Y 0DZ
An Hachette UK Company

www.hachette.co.uk
www.asterix.com
www.hachettechildrens.co.uk

 Asterix and Obelix

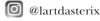 @lartdasterix

NIGHT IS ABOUT TO FALL OVER THE VILLAGE WHEN THREE MYSTERIOUS HORSEMEN APPROACH THE CHIEF'S HUT...

NOW, THAT'S AN IMPORTANT MEETING!

PEEP PEEP
PEEP
PEEP
COOOT

1A

I RECOGNISE THEM! IT'S MONOLITHIX AND SIDEKIX, TWO ARVERNI CHIEFS.

VITALSTATISTIX AND I FOUGHT ALONGSIDE THEM. THEY WERE LIEUTENANTS TO VERCINGETORIX.

TO WHO?

VERCINGETORIX... SINCE HIS DEFEAT AT ALESIA NO ONE SAYS HIS NAME OUT LOUD!

GREETINGJ TO 40U, VITALSHTATISHTIX!

THE MEMBERJ OF RAF* SHALUTE 40U!

POC

*REJISHTANSHE BY ARVERNI FIGHTERJ

1B

THISH IJ ADRENALIN, VERSHINGETORIX'J ONLY DAUGHTER.

POC

?!

SHAY HELLO, ADRENALIN.

'LO

BY TOUTATIS! I DIDN'T KNOW VER... VERCINGETORIX HAD A DAUGHTER!

NO ONE KNOWJ BUT USH!

THE GENERALISSHIMO WAJ VERY DISHCREET ABOUT HIJ PRIVATE LIFE*...

POC

*HISTORIANS REMAIN DIVIDED ABOUT HIS DESCENDANTS TO THIS DAY.

BEFORE SHURRENDERING TO SHAEJAR AT ALEJIA, HE ENTRUSHTED THE CHILD TO USH...

2A

HE GAVE HER HIJ TORC*, SHAYING SHE MUSHT ALWAYJ REJISHT CONQUESHT IN HIJ NAME AND SHTAY FREE...

*HONORARY GAULISH NECKWEAR

WITH HELP FROM OUR SHUPPORTERJ WE THEN BROKE THROUGH ENEMY LINEJ WITH HER.

THE RESHT IJ HISHTORY...

OUCH!

CLANG!

WE'RE HERE TO ENTRUSHT HER TO YOU BECAUJE THE ROMANJ HAVE BEEN SHEARCHING FOR HER EVER SHINSHE.

POC!

...

PFF

YOUR ANTLERJ!

2B

YOU SHEE THERE WAJ A TRAITOR IN OUR MIDSHT! THE TRACKER BINJWATCHFLIX WAJ ON SHAEJAR'S PAYROLL...

WE KNOW HE REPORTED BACK TO SHAEJAR...

WHAT DO YOU MEAN? THAT TORC COULD BE A SYMBOL TO ENCOURAGE MORE REVOLTS, BY JUPITER!

BRING IT TO ME AND BRING THE GIRL TOO, WE'LL MAKE A PROPER ROMAN OF HER*... IF YOU SUCCEED YOU SHALL BE SCOUT LEADER IN MY ELITE UNITS!

WITH A XIITH MONTH BONUS?

*IT WAS COMMON PRACTICE TO FORCIBLY 'ROMANISE' SOME HOSTAGES.

THE TRAITOR'J BEEN TRACKING USH ALL THISH TIME, SHO WE ALWAYJ HAVE TO KEEP THE CHILD HIDDEN!

YEAH, LIKE, WHATEVER, GET OUT YOUR LYRES, WHY DON'T YOU!

3A

UM... THAT'S STRANGE, SHE DOESN'T HAVE YOUR ARVERNI ACCENT!

THAT'SH BECAUJE SHE SHPENT A LONG TIME HIDDEN IN LUTESHIA, A LITTLE PLASHE BEYOND NEMESHOSH*

*CLERMONT-FERRAND

GAUL IJN'T SHAFE NOW, WE'RE TAKING HER TO LONDINIUM* IN BRITAIN WHERE SHAEJAR WON'T THINK OF LOOKING FOR HER...

*LONDON

WE'RE OFF TO JOIN OUR FORSHEJ ON THE COASHT. WE'LL BE BACK SHOON WITH A SHIP...

THE PORTSH ARE INFESHTED WITH ROMANJ, SHE'LL BE NISHE AND SHAFE HERE IN THE MEANTIME...

I PROMISE WE'LL LOOK AFTER HER, MONOLITHIX, YOU HAVE MY INDOMITABLE WORD.

THANK YOU, VI-TALSHTAT-ISHTIX.

BE A GOOD GIRL, ADRENALIN, YOUR DADDIESJ WILL BE BACK!

SHMACK

NNG

DON'T YOU WORRY, WE'LL TAKE GOOD CARE OF HER!

BUT BE CAREFUL, ADRENALIN'J RESPONSHE IJ TO RUN! SHE'J A BOLTER!

3B

"STRONG AS AN AUROCHS!"

"DISHCREET AJ A MOLE!"

PFFOOOT!

DON'T BE SHAD, SHIDEKIX!

WE'LL BE BACK SHOON WITH THE RAFSH. YOU'LL SHEE OUR FLEDGLING AGAIN!

I KNOW... BUT IT'SH HARD. SHNIFF! I CAN'T HELP MYSHELF!

YOU COME WITH AUNTIE IMPEDIMENTA, ADRENALIN! SHE'LL SHOW YOU YOUR ROOM!

SOMETHING TROUBLING YOU, CHIEF?

COME WITH ME. LET'S GO AND SEE GETAFIX.

A DAUGHTER? INTERESTING! I DIDN'T KNOW VERCIN...

VERCINGETORIX WAS VERY DISCREET ABOUT HIS PRIVATE LIFE!

WHO?

RIGHT, YOU KNOW EVERYTHING NOW! YOU AND OBELIX WILL BE HER MINDERS, NOTHING MUST HAPPEN TO HER. IT'S OUR HISTORIC DUTY TO PROTECT THE GIRL: OUR CREDIBILITY IS AT STAKE.

BUT BE CAREFUL: SHE'S A BOLTER.

MEANWHILE IN THE SLEEPING TOTORUM CAMP...

ZZZ

?! WHO ARE YOU AND HOW DID YOU GET IN HERE WITH YOUR HORSE?

MY NAME IS BINJWATCHFLIX, I'M SILENT LIKE ALL TRACKERS AND DISCREET LIKE ALL TRAITORS...

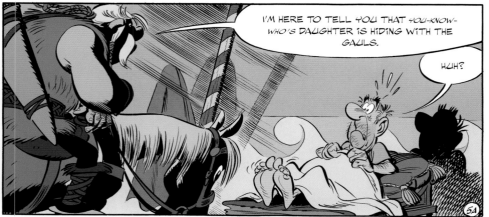

I'M HERE TO TELL YOU THAT *YOU-KNOW-WHO'S* DAUGHTER IS HIDING WITH THE GAULS.

HUH?

YOU HEARD ME! CAESAR HAS TOLD ME TO CAPTURE HER SO HE CAN MAKE A ROMAN OF HER.

WHO?

I MUST GO TO GESOCRIBATUM* TO WARN THE FLEET. THEY MUST STOP HER ESCAPING BY SEA! AND YOU MUST STOP HER ESCAPING THROUGH THE FOREST.

*LE CONQUET

AND BE CAREFUL, SHE'S A BOLTER!

ZZZ

ZZZ

ZZZ

WHOSE DAUGHTER?

NEXT MORNING...

WHERE **WERE** YOU? SHE'S GONE TO THE **MARKET** WiTH iMPEDiMENTA!

GO ON, GO! AND DON'T TAKE YOUR EYES OFF HER AGAiN!

IT'S JUST I'VE GOT THIS MENHIR TO DELIVER AS WELL AND...

LATER, OBELiX!

NAH, GiRLS' CLOTHES ARE RUBBiSH! I'D WAY RATHER DRESS LiKE A GOTH!

YES, YES, WE'LL SEE ABOUT THAT.

AND I DON'T NEED LOOKiNG AFTER!

TOO LATE, YOU'LL HAVE LOTS OF FRIENDS NOW.

THE DEAD SPiT OF HER FATHER, VERCiNGETORiX!

WHO I KNEW VERY WELL, AS iT HAPPENS!

AND WHAT'S THAT ROUND HER NECK?

HER DADDY'S TORC!

SHE'S A SULKY LITTLE THING!

PROBABLY ALL *TORC* AND NO ACTION.

AND A HELL OF A STRATEGIST! REMEMBER THE GERGOVIA VICTORY!

GREAT ATMOSPHERE! HE GATHERED QUITE A CROWD THAT DAY!

A MAN WiTH A PROPER MOUSTACHE WHO STOOD UP TO JULIUS, LiKE US!

AND WiTHOUT ANY POTION.

WHOSE DAUGHTER?

VERCiNGETORiX'S!!!

SH

UNHYGIENIX SEAFOO

MEANWHILE AT TOTORUM...

DO WE UNDERSTAND EACH OTHER?

YOUR CENTURION WILL BE RETIRING ON THE IDES OF MAIUS*

*15TH MAY

AND THAT MEANS DON'T GO PROVOKING ALESIA II IN MY LAST MONTH!

SO WHETHER OR NOT SHE'S THINGY'S DAUGHTER, WE DON'T KNOW ABOUT HER, HAVEN'T HEARD A THING, DO A BIT OF PATROLLING AND LET THE OTHERS DEAL WITH IT, CAPEESH?

AT EASE!

GOOD PLAN!

EXCELLENT PLAN!

VERY CLEVER!

REMARKABLE TACTICIAN!

THE TROOPS IN GESOCRIBATUM HAVE BEEN INFORMED. SHE CAN'T GET AWAY FROM ME NOW!

AAAAAH! SHE'S DONE A RUNNER!

NO SHE HASN'T, DON'T BE SO SILLY!

SHE'S AT THE QUARRY WITH THE OTHER YOUNGSTERS. ASTERIX AND OBELIX ARE KEEPING AN EYE ON HER.

I DON'T LIKE THEM PLAYING IN MY QUARRY. I'M ALWAYS WORRIED THEY'LL CHIP ONE OF MY MENHIRS...

MAYBE SHE'S PLANNING TO RUN AWAY?

D'YOU THINK?

GO AND MINGLE DISCREETLY WITH THE GANG TO FIND OUT!

HUH? WHY ME?

YOU'RE MORE LIKE A TEENAGER THAN ME.

AH.

♪

WHO'S THAT?

OBELIX AND DOGMATIX.

IT'S FINE! THEY WORK HERE!

YOUR TORC'S WELL COOL!

YEAH, 'CEPT CAESAR WANTS TO GET HIS HANDS ON IT.

HE ALSO WANTS TO HAVE ME, LIKE, KIDNAPPED AND BROUGHT UP AS A ROMAN.

MEH! YEAH AND MY PARENTS WANT ME TO BE A FISHMONGER LIKE THEM.

AND MINE WANT ME TO BE A BLACKSMITH, SO DON'T EVEN!

WELL, I'VE ALWAYS WANTED TO DELIVER MENHIRS.

? ? ? ?

UGH! MENHIRS ARE PANTS!

LOSER! YOU'RE JUST INTO BOAR, MENHIRS, POTION AND MORE BOAR. YOU COULD BORE FOR GAUL!

WHAT? BUT THE POTION'S VERY GOOD, AND SO'S WILD BOAR!

YOU'RE JOKING! WE DONT EVEN KNOW WHAT THE OLD MAN PUTS IN THAT POTION!

WOAH, MAN, PRETTY GALLING, 'EY!

YEAH! YOU NEVER KNOW, THAT COULD BE WHAT MADE YOU OBESE!

PFRR

AS FOR THE BOAR, THE RATE THEY'RE BEING HUNTED THEY'LL ALL BE GONE SOON!

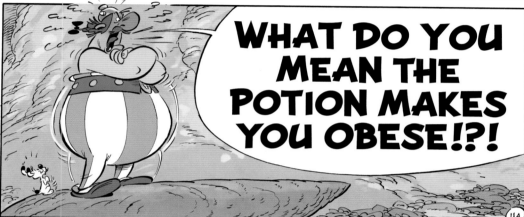

WHAT DO YOU MEAN THE POTION MAKES YOU OBESE!?!

AND BOOM! WHEREVER I GO, ALESIA BREAKS OUT ALL OVER AGAIN... I CAN'T TAKE IT ANYMORE!

LET'S GO ROUND TO SEE CACOFONIX, AT LEAST HE UNDERSTANDS US.

YEAH, NO ONE WANTS HIM AROUND EITHER!

WE LOVE HIS DISTURBING SONGS.

IT'S OK, OBELIX. YOU CAN GET DOWN NOW.

BOOHOOHOOHOO! THE OTHER TEENAGERS DON'T LIKE ME !!!

AA-OOOOO

THE NEXT DAY...

NO! I'M NOT WEARING GIRLS' TUNICS! THEY'RE LAME AND THEY DON'T GO WITH MY TORC!

? ?

?

NOT EVEN THE BLACK ONE?

WITH STUDS?

COME ON! WE NEED TO FOLLOW HER DISCREETLY, OBELIX!

I'M FINE WITH THAT...

... BUT IT'S GOING TO BE DIFFICULT TO KEEP LOOKING NATURAL!

? ? ?

AT THE FISHMONGER'S, OVER THERE!

BE GENTLE AND DON'T UPSET HER! THE TEENAGE YEARS ARE A DIFFICULT TIME. FORCE WON'T GET YOU ANYWHERE. REMEMBER, TALK AND NOTHING ELSE!

GETAFIX IS RIGHT. DOGMATIX AND I HAVE ALWAYS TALKED A LOT, HAVEN'T WE, DOGMATIX?

WOOF

HEY! YOU COMING TO THE QUARRY WITH ME?

NO, BLINIX! YOU'RE NOT GOING OFF WITH LITTLE MISS VERCINGETORIX TILL YOU'VE DONE THESE MUSSELS!

BUT, DAD, I HAVEN'T GOT THE STRENGTH FOR MORE MUSSELS!

UGH! ALL THIS ARGUING, IT'S ALWAYS ABOUT ME!

WHEREVER I GO, THE MINUTE SOMEONE SAYS MY NAME PEOPLE START FIGHTING! ADRENALIN – FIGHT!

NO, CHEER UP! ANYWAY, PEOPLE HERE JUST FIGHT OVER ANYTHING.

IT'S NORMAL.

...CEPT WHEN VEY DON'T LIKE EACH OTHER, OBVS!

YES, I KNOW! MY TWO ARVERNI DADS ARE THE SAME. ALL THEY CAN THINK ABOUT IS FIGHTING AND RECONQUERING GAUL WITH ME.

I'M SO OVER PEOPLE USING ME AND MY TORC TO START WARS. I CAN'T KEEP MY FEELINGS AMPHORAED UP ANY LONGER.

THAT'S IT THEN! I SET OFF AT NIGHTFALL!

PERFECT! COME ON, NOSFERATUS, WE KNOW ENOUGH!

BUT... WHERE WILL YOU GO?

I'LL GO AND HELP CHILDREN WITH NO PARENTS, LIKE ME. I'LL TAKE THEM TO A FARAWAY ISLAND, BEYOND THE KNOWN WORLD, WHERE THE ROMANS WON'T EVER FIND ME!

VAT'S AWESOME!

OBELIX QUARRY CAUTION MENHIRS TURNING

ONCE WHEN I DID A BUNK IN LUTECIA, AN OLD GREEK SAILOR CALLED TAYKINTHEMYKONOS TOLD ME ABOUT THIS ISLAND. IT'S CALLED THULE* AND EVEN CAESAR DOESN'T KNOW IT EXISTS!

*A LEGENDARY ISLAND MENTIONED BY THE GREEK HERODOTUS IN THE 5TH CENTURY BC.

WELL SAID, BY TOUTATIS! **LET'S ALL GO VERE!**

UMM... MY DAD'LL NEVER AGREE TO THAT!

OURS NEITHER! ...YOU KNOW HE WON'T, NOT IN THE MIDDLE OF THE MUSSEL SEASON!

NO WORRIES! I'LL BE FINE ON MY OWN... BUT IF YOU COULD HELP ME GET OUT OF THE VILLAGE...

VAT'S EASY! I'VE GOT A PLAN!

DO YOU KNOW SOMETHING, ASTERIX, I'M BEGINNING TO THINK I PREFER MISSIONS ABROAD...

WHERE IN GAUL HAVE THEY GONE?

... WE GET TO SEE PLACES, TRY LOCAL SPECIALITI

WATCH OUT! THEY'RE COMING BACK THIS WAY!

THOSE SHIFTY FACES... LOOKS LIKE THEY'RE PLOTTING SOMETHING!

SHOULD WE STILL BE LOOKING NATURAL?

NO! WE'RE GOING TO ASK THE CHIEF TO GUARD EVERY EXIT POINT! ...

WHILE TENSION MOUNTS IN THE VILLAGE, A FEW CABLE LENGTHS AWAY...

THE WIND'S DROPPED, CAPTAIN! WE'VE STOPPED!

?!

SHIVER ME TIMBERS! WHAT DID YOU SAY?

AAAARGH! BECALMED ONLY A COUPLE OF FATHOMS SHORT OF THE GAULISH VILLAGE!

BAH! EX MALO BONUM! LET'S USE THE OPPORTUNITY TO FILL UP ON FRESH WATER!

WATER! WHEN THE HOLD'S FULL OF PLONK FROM THAT PHOENICIAN TRADER!?

YES, ABOUT THAT! LOOK AT THE EFFECT THAT CAVE-PAINT-STRIPPER IS HAVING ON OUR MEN!

KARMA KARMA KARMA KARMA KARMA PHOENICIAN WINDS COME AND GO, THEY COME AND GO

LAAAA BOHEEEEME

ENOUGH! ALRIGHT, ALRIGHT! WE'LL SEND OUT A ROWING BOAT AT NIGHTFALL!

♪♪ WHEN THE WORLD SEEMS TO SHINE LIKE YOU'VE HAD TOO MUCH WINE THAT'S AMPHORAE!

SILENCE ALL OF YOU! I LIKE TO KEEP A TIGHT SHIP!!!

DON'T GEDDIT

NIGHT HAS FALLEN. TO AVOID ANY ADRENALIN LOSS, BACKTOBASIX IS STANDING AN UNUSUAL KIND OF GUARD, FACING TOWARDS THE VILLAGE...

HYPERVIGILANT THANKS TO THE DRUID'S MAGIC POTION, HE WON'T EVEN BLINK...

PSST

WHAT ARE YOU DOING HERE, CHILDREN? NOT IN BED YET?

WE'RE KEEPING WATCH LIKE YOU, BACKTOBASIX!

BUT IT'S TIRING! SO WE THOUGHT WITH A DROP OF POTION...

YOUNG MAN! AT YOUR AGE! THAT'S NOT ALLOWED. WHAT WOULD YOUR PARENTS SAY?

THEY'LL NEVER KNOW! GO ON! JUST A DROP!

DEARIE ME! ALRIGHT! HALF A TOT THEN! AND JUST FOR THE TWO BIGGER BOYS... YOU'RE LUCKY, I REMEMBER BEING YOUNG...

SHE'S DONE A RUNNER!

VERCINGETORIX'S

DAUGHTER!

HUH?

WH... WHO?

WHO HAS?

SO I GO INTO HER BEDROOM AND SHE'S NOT THERE!

SHE'S NOT IN THE VILLAGE!

WE'VE LOOKED EVERYWHERE!

I... I DON'T UNDERSTAND, CHIEF! I DIDN'T LEAVE MY POST!

THE SESTERTIUS ALWAYS STOPS WITH ME IN THIS PLACE...

SUCH A SENSITIVE GIRL! WE SHOULD HAVE KNOWN THIS WOULD HAPPEN.

SOUND THE HORN FOR A GATHERING!

SHE MUSTN'T GET INTO THE ROMANS' CLUTCHES!

POOR CHILD!

COCK-A-DOODLE-DOOO

BY TOUTATIS! THIS IS WHAT HAPPENS IF YOU DON'T DO A JOB YOURSELF!

EVERYONE TO THE FOREST! SPLIT INTO TEAMS!

YOU TWO THERE, WITH US!

OKAY!

OKAY!

WHOOOOSH

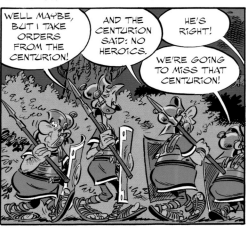

23

THE WORLD HAS CHANGED, AND YOU PEOPLE, YOU BACKWARD INDOMITABLE PEOPLE DON'T SEEM TO UNDERSTAND CHANGE MEANS CHANGE! THE FUTURE BELONGS TO CAESAR AND TO HIS FOLLOWERS.

NONSENSE!

PLAFF!

BY CERNUNNOS, THE HORNED GOD! THE GIRL'S MANAGED TO SLIP AWAY!

CATCH UP WITH HER, NOSFERATUS!

ADRENALIN! COO-EE!

YOU CAN SHOUT OUT LOUD, OBELIX!

ADRENALIN! COO-EE!

WHAT SHOULD WE DO?

BE BRAVE! AND FOLLOW OUR INSTRUCTIONS!

THE GAULS!

SEEK, DOGMATIX, SEEK!

WELL, IF IT'S FOR THINGY'S DAUGHTER...

WE DON'T KNOW A THING!

ANYWAY, WE DIDN'T EVEN KNOW THINGY HAD A DAUGHTER, SO THERE!

RRR

POFF POFF POFF

Light signals to starboard, Daddykinsus!

DON'T CALL ME 'DADDYKINSUS', LUDWIKAMADEUS! WE'RE NOT AT THE VILLA NOW!

IT'S THE TRACKER SIGNALLING: THE RUNAWAY'S TRYING TO ESCAPE BY SEA. WE MUST INTERCEPT ANY SUSPECT VESSELS IN THE AREA ...

Can I command this manoeuvre, Daddykinsus?

WE'LL SEE ABOUT THAT! MEANWHILE, GO AND SET THE RHYTHM FOR THE REMIGES*

*ROWERS

Yaaaaau! That's awesome!

Thanks, Daddykinsus!

Yo, you rem' guys!!! Let's push the boat out!

BOM tchack-a-tchack BOM BOM BOM tack-a-tack tchack

YOU SEE, SNOEXCUSUS, IT'S NOT ALWAYS EASY BRINGING UP A LITTLE GOTH AS A ROMAN.

COMPLICATED AS INFERNUM, THESE BARBARIAN RHYTHMS!

26

CALL THIS FRESH WATER?

IT'S HER, CAPTAIN! SHE FOLLOWED US ALL THE WAY FROM THE FOREST...

COULD WE TAKE HER HOSTAGE?

TAKE HER HOSTAGE?!? WHEN WE'RE A MENHIR'S THROW FROM THE GAULISH VILLAGE?!?

I'M NOT FROM THE VILLAGE. I'M ADRENALIN, DAUGHTER OF THE GREAT ARVERNI CHIEF VERCINGETORIX!

?!

VERMINHYDROLIX? WHO'S THAT?

VERCINGETORIX? A GENERAL: RENOWNED FOR A BATTLE HE LOST TO THE ROMANS BUT I'M NOT SURE I REMEMBER WHERE...

OH, AND HE'S A GENERAL? TOO RISKY! THROW HER OVERBOARD!

23A

BUT IT MIGHT BE WORTH KEEPING HER AS A HOSTAGE! THE ARVERNI ARE WEALTHY NEGOTIATORS...

THEY SELL WINE!

WE COULD ASK A HUGE RANSOM IN WINE!

IT WOULD MEAN WE COULD SAVE ON FRESH WATER!

FOR ME THAT WOULD BE FORMI—HIC— FORMIDABLE!

THE TRAIL STOPS HERE.

I'LL GO ON ALONE, NOSFERATUS! GO AND WAIT FOR ME AT THE ROMAN CAMP!

23B

TAKE ME WITH YOU! I CAN'T HANDLE THEM ANYMORE, DON'T YOU GET IT?

WHO... WHO DO YOU MEAN?

THE ARVERNI! THE GAULS! THE ROMANS!

THEY HANG ON MY TUNIC STRINGS AND I NEED SOME SPACE!

YOU KNOW, I'VE GOT A SOFT SPOT FOR THAT KID.

ME TOO, SHE REMINDS ME OF MY OWN LITTLE GIRLY...

I'VE GOT ONE JUST LIKE HER IN MASSILIA, CARTHAGE, ALEXANDRIA...

THAT'S ENOUGH! LET'S THROW HER IN THE DRINK!

FRESH OR SALTY, CAP—HIC—TAIN?

LOOK OUT! SHE'S GETTING AWAY!

SHE'S RACING UP THE MAST!

THAT'S WHAT YOU CALL—HIC!—AN ADRENALIN RUSH!

GET DOWN FROM THIS MAST IMMEDIATELY!

THAT'S MY MAST, CAPTAIN.

NOPE! AND YOU SHOULD BE ASHAMED OF YOURSELF, LEAVING CHILDREN IN EVERY PORT!

?!

OH!

WHOOOSH

THE WIND'S GETTING UP!

?!

WELL, I'LL BE BLOWED! LET'S MAKE A GAULISH EXIT! EVERYONE TO YOUR POSTS! RAISE THE SAILS!

SPEAKING OF POSTS, CAPTAIN...

BE QUIET AND GET ON WITH IT!

SEEK, DOGMATIX!

SNIFF SNIFF

THE PIRATE SHIP.

ADRENALIN! THEY'VE KIDNAPPED HER!

POOR THINGS!

WAH! WAH!

HEH HEH! WE'VE GOT A GOOD LEAD! THEY'LL NEVER CATCH UP!

WE'VE MANAGED TO SHAKE OFF THE GAULS FOR ONCE!

HOORAY!

25A

TO THE VILLAGE! WE NEED TO TELL THE CHIEF AND FIND A BOAT!

WELL, THERE'S MY DAD'S BUT IT'S BEING REPAIRED...

...BY MY DAD!

!

EEEEE

SOMEONE'S COMING!

REMEMBER OUR INSTRUCTIONS!

NO PROVOCATIVE MOVES! STAY PUT...

BONG

OBELIX?

RIGHT, THAT'S THAT! POINTLESS BUT STRESS-BUSTING!

...STICK TOGETHER...

25C

WELL, THAT'S ANOTHER FINE MESS, BY TOUTATIS! HELL IS EMPTY AND ALL THE DEVILS ARE ON THAT SHIP!

BY ACIONNA, LET'S HOPE THERE ISN'T A TEMPEST!

TAKE CARE OF HER! SHE'S A PLEASURE BOAT I'VE BEEN SAVING FOR MY RETIREMENT!

The Phoenix

BUT IT WASN'T ME, IT WAS CRABSTIX WHO HAD THE PLAN TO GET ADRENALIN OU

WHAT? HOW DARE YOU ACCUSE YOUR LITTLE BROTHER?!

ENOUGH!

IF THAT'S THE WAY IT IS, BLINIX AND SELFIPIX, YOU CAN GO WITH ASTERIX AND OBELIX TO HELP THEM CLEAR UP!

ERR...

YES! YES!

WE'LL CLEAR UP! WE'RE UP FOR THAT!

WE'LL TAKE CARE OF THE TRAITOR! BRING US BACK VERCINGETORIX'S DAUGHTER!

WE SHALL, CHIEF!

AND AS SOON AS WE'VE DONE THAT, I'LL DELIVER MY MENHIR!

AND I REALLY HOPE THE ARVERNI DON'T COME BACK TOO SOON!

MEANWHILE...

ONE THING PUTSH MY MIND AT RESHT, SHIDEKIX, AND THAT'SH KNOWING THE GIRL'J IN SHAFE HANDJ!

SHAME HERE, MONLITHIX.

WE'LL SHTOP OFF TO PICK HER UP AND THEN SHET SHAIL FOR LONDINIUM.

AND IT'SH FROM THERE THAT RAF AND THEIR ALLIEJ THE BRITONJ WILL LAUNCH THEIR MAJOR OFFENSHIVE AGAINSHT THE ROMAN OCCUPATION!

CAPTAIN PEACENIX, FREE GAUL WILL DEMONSHTRATE ITSH BOUNDLESH GRATITUDE TO YOU!

NO WORRIES, BROTHER! IT'S A BLAST, MAKES A CHANGE FROM THE BULBS AND SEEDS I USUALLY TRANSPORT!

YOU MAY SAY I'M A DREAMER BUT, LIKE YOU, I BELIEVE THERE'LL BE PEACE AGAIN SOMEDAY...

THERE'LL BE NO COUNTRIES, ROMANS AND GAULS WILL LIVE AS ONE, SOWING FLOWER SEEDS TOGETHER ALL OVER THE WORLD...

27a

MONOLITHIX, THISH PEACENIX IJ SHTRANGE. HIJ IDEAJ COULD DEMOBILIZE OUR MEN...

YOU'RE RIGHT, LET'SH CHANGE THAT! GOOD MEN, REMEMBER...

"SHTRONG AJ AN AUROCHS!!!"

"DISHCREET AJ A MOLE!"

THAT'S BETTER.

?

STILL NOTHING!

SEEK, DOGMATIX, SEEK!

?

SHALL WE TELL THEM, BLINIX?

LET'S TELL THEM, SELFIPIX!

27c

UM... THE EFFECTS OF THE POTION ARE, LIKE, WEARING OFF...

IF WE COULD MAYBE HAVE, LIKE, ANOTHER TOT?

I DON'T KNOW IF THAT'S ALLOWED?

?!

YES BUT NO BUT YES BUT! HOW COME THE OTHER TEENAGERS CAN HAVE IT AND NOT ME?

WELL, BECAUSE YOU'RE NOT A TEENAGER, OBELIX!

MAKE UP YOUR MIND!

IN THE QUARRY THE OTHER DAY YOU WERE THE ONE WHO...

NO, IT'S FINE, I GET IT! HIS SELF-IMPORTANCE MISTER ASTERIX LIKES THE OTHER TEENAGERS MORE!

OKAY, FINE! HALF A TOT BUT JUST TO MAKE YOU ROW FASTER!

SICK! I SWEAR WE WON'T TELL OUR PARENTS!

WHATEVER! DON'T EVEN KNOW WHAT'S IN IT SO AM I BOVVERED?

WOOOHHHHH

THEY'LL SOON SEE WHEN THEY'RE OBESE!

THERE! THAT'S EKONOMIKRISIS'S SHIP!*

*AS SEEN IN ASTERIX THE GLADIATOR

THE PIRATES? OH YES, WE'VE SEEN THEM, ASTERIX! THEY TOOK OUR WHOLE CARGO OF WINE IN AMPHORAE HEADED FOR THE GAULISH MARKET!

IT'S BAD FOR BUSINESS FOR A SAILOR TO LOSE HIS AMPHORA!

GLUG GLUG

BLUE SKY THINKING, BOYS! WE NEED TO ABSORB OUR LOSSES AND GET BACK ON AN EVEN KEEL!

SO THAT EXPLAINS THE HUNDRED MILLION AMPHORAE WASHED UP ON THE SHORE!

WHAT ARE THE GAULS LIKE?!

A THROWAWAY SOCIETY! THEY CONSUME AND THEN, BOOM, THEY THROW AWAY!

AND PLUS, LOOK AT THEIR OVER-CONSUMPTION OF BOAR!

WHAT'VE YOU GOT AGAINST OVERCONSUMING BOAR?

OBELIX! CALM DOWN!

THEY STARTED IT! THEY KEEP WINDING ME UP!

ENOUGH!

HURRY UP! THESE AMPHORAE WILL LEAD US TO THE PIRATES. WE MUST SAVE ADRENALIN!

BY TOUTATIS, THIS IS THE LAST TIME I TRAVEL WITH THREE TEENAGERS!

NUH NUH NUH NUH

MEANWHILE, ON THE PIRATE SHIP...

NO WAY! NOT COMING DOWN! I HEARD YOU! I KNOW YOU WANT TO SELL ME!

WHAT SHALL WE DO, CAPTAIN? SHE'S TAKEN MY POSITION, IT'S NOT A VERY ELEVATED POSITION, BUT I LIKE IT!

WELL, I THINK SHE'S FUN, SHE'S GOT A BIT OF CHARACTER!

WHAT IF WE ADOPTED HER AS OUR MASCOT?

YOU REALLY GET MY GOAT SOMETIMES

WE COULD BROADEN HER EDUCATION!

IT WOULD BRING A BIT OF REFINEMENT TO THE SHIP...

BEHIND YOU!

BEHIND YOU!

?

HUH? WHAT IS IT NOW?

34

WE'VE CAUGHT UP WITH THEM! COME ON, OBELIX! LET'S GO!

AND STAY NATURAL, I KNOW!

GLUG GLUG GLUG

UM...

WHAT ABOUT US?

NUH NUH NUH-NUH NUH! YOU'RE TOO YOUNG! STAY HERE AND LOOK AFTER DOGMATIX!

WOOF

SEEING AS THE POTION MAKES YOU OBESE!

THAT'LL DO, OBELIX, STOP GRUMBLING!

DANGER TO STARBOARD!

PAFF

WHERE'S THE GIRL?

WHICH GIRL?

GIRL?

GIRL?

?!

ADRENALIN!

YES, AND WE'VE LOOKED AFTER HER VERY VERY WELL!

I'D EVEN SAY SHE'S BECOME A BIT OF A MASCOT!

WHO IN THE KNOWN WORLD IS HE?

A FREELANCER!

THE SORT WHO DISCREDITS A WHOLE PROFESSION!

IT'S BINJWATCHFLIX, THE TRAITOR! AND YOU CAN LEAVE WITH HIM!

NOW COME ON, ADRENALIN! THE WHOLE VILLAGE IS WORRIED, IT WAS NAUGHTY TO RUN AWAY!

OH, FOR PYTHIA'S SAKE!* WHAT AM I, THE MOST WANTED KID IN ARMORICA?

*HIGH PRIESTESS AT THE TEMPLE OF APOLLO.

I'VE DECIDED ME AND MY CREW ARE GOING TO HEAD FOR THULE!

YOUR CREW?

THULE! THE ISLAND OF PLENTY REFERRED TO BY THE ANCIENTS?

THEY SAY IT'S FAR BEYOND THE LAND OF THE PICTS.

AND FULL OF WELCOMING CALLYPIGIAN GIANTESSES!

...THE GROUND IS STREWN WITH GOLD!

...THE AIR SMELLS OF JASMINE!

AND THE RIVERS FLOW WITH WINE!

TAKE ME ALOOOONG!

"OMNE IGNOTUM PRO MAGNIFICO". THEY EVEN SAY OLD PEOPLE'S TEETH AND LEGS GROW BACK OVER THERE!

?!

32A

OH, I'M CRAZY FOR THULE!

IT'S THE MASCOT'S LATEST CRAZE!

LET'S ALL JOIN THE CRAZE!

YES, CRAZY NOT TO!

SHIVER ME TIMBERS, IT'S A MUTINY!

THESE PIRATES ARE CRAZY.

ALL I CAN SAY IS WHEN IT COMES TO LEADERSHIP, ADRENALIN'S DEFINITELY A VERCINGETORIX...

LISTEN, WE MAY HAVE HAD OUR DIFFERENCES BUT WE BASICALLY UNDERSTAND EACH OTHER, RIGHT. SINK US, DO SOMETHING, BUT PLEASE LET'S JUST GET BACK TO NORMAL...

?

?

BOM BOM BOM

32B

36

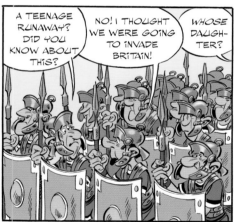

THE "CORVUS" (CROW), A MUCH-FEARED HOOKED GANGWAY WHICH CAN HARPOON THE ENEMY BRIDGE...

SO THAT TROOPS CAN FLOOD ABOARD IT...

CRACK

CLEVER IDEA!

THE ROMAN ARMY IS NOT WELL DISPOSED TO NAVAL COMBAT, BUT THIS SIMPLE DEVICE...

PROVIDES CONDITIONS MORE LIKE THE LAND-BASED COMBAT AT WHICH THE ROMANS EXCEL...

SO, HOW ARE YOU FINDING THESE SEA-GOING ROMANS?

OH, I'VE TAKEN THE WIND OUT OF THEIR SAILS!

SHLACK

41

DO YOU SEE WHAT I SEE, BLINIX?

A CHANCE TO REDEEM OURSELVES, SELFIPIX!

POC

GRRR

LET'S FOLLOW HER...

...AND STAY NATURAL, I KNOW!

PLONK

MY TORC! HE TOOK MY TORC!

OUCH!

CROCK

SPLOOSH!

RRR

BLB BLB BLB

YOU STILL HAVEN'T GOT ME!

ROME! ROME!

GLORY TO CAESAR!

DON'T BOTHER! THERE'S NOWHERE HE CAN GO!

I NEVER FORGET A PLACE. I'LL BE BACK FOR THE TORC!

AND NOTHING CAN STOP ME.

MISSION ACCOMPLISHED! LET'S GO HOME, MY DEAR OLD OBELIX!

OKAY, BUT THIS TIME DOGMATIX AND ME ARE ROWING.

WOOF

AH HA HA HA HAAAA!

THEY'VE ALL GONE! IT ALL WORKED OUT! WE WORE THEM DOWN IN THE END, BOYS!

SNIFF! SHAME! SHE WAS A TREASURE, AND HER ISLAND...

SHE MAY BE THE FACE I CAN'T FORGET!

39A

CAPTAIN, THE WATER'S GETTING IN WHERE THEY TORE OUT THE MAST...

GLB GLUB GLB BLB

SO ABOUT MY POSITION, THEN?

BLB BLB BLB GLB

AND AFTER A SMOOTH CROSSING...

TOUTATIS BE PRAISED! HERE YOU ARE AT LAST!

THE RAF BOYS ARE HERE AND THEY'RE NOT HAPPY!

WE COULD HAVE REBUILT GERGOVIA THREE TIMES OVER WHILE WE WERE WAITING!

39B

I SHEE! SHO YOU DID A RUNNER AGAIN DID YOU, LITTLE MISSHY?!

AND WHERE'J YOUR TORC, IF YOU PLEAJE?

WHAT ABOUT YOU? WHERE WERE YOU WHILE I WAS BEING KIDNAPPED BY THE TRACKER?

BUT YOU DON'T CARE TWO SESTERCES ABOUT THAT!

ALL THAT MATTERS TO YOU IS MY TORC! WELL, IT'S UNDERWATER NOW!

SO THERE!

POC

DEAL WITH IT! YOU CAN RECONQUER THE COUNTRY WITHOUT ME!

SHTRONG AJ AN AUROCHS!

DISHCREET AJ A MOLE!

THAT'SH RIGHT! THAT'SH RIGHT!

SLAM

YOU TWO, FOLLOW HER!

YESH, WE KNOW.

VERY SHTRANGE! I GET THE FEELING ADRENALIN DOEJN'T LIKE A FIGHT!

BOOHOOHOO! HOW DID WE GET THE POOR CHILD'J UPBRINGING SHO WRONG?!

OH, DON'T DESHPAIR!

THE MAIN THING IS SHE'S GOT PLENTY OF CHARACTER!

SHE'S HEADING FOR THE PONTOON...

HI! I'M ADRENALIN... NICE SHIP, IS IT YOURS?

HEY! I'M PEACENIX...

YEP, RIGHT NOW IT'S ARVERNIS, BUT I USUALLY TRANSPORT FLOWERS AND BULBS FROM ISLAND TO ISLAND...

OH REALLY, IN YOUR SHIP? FROM ISLAND TO ISLAND?

OBELIX, MY FRIEND, DO YOU SEE WHAT I SEE?

SHALL I MINGLE DISCREETLY?

NO, LET'S GO BACK! SOMETHING TELLS ME EVERYTHING'S FALLING INTO PLACE.

OH? HOW COME?

YOU'RE RIGHT, GETAFIX, WE WERE BLINDED BY OUR WARRIOR SHPIRIT!

IT'SH OBVIOUSH ADRENALIN'J NEVER GOING TO WAGE THISH WAR WITH USH...

IT'SH MY FAULT! I SHOULD NEVER HAVE TAUGHT HER TO WIELD AN AXE!

DON'T BE SHILLY, IT WAJ ME, I WAJ TOO SHTRICT! ...

DON'T DO THISH AND SHTOP DOING THAT...

NO MATERNAL INSTINCT, OBVIOUSLY!

BONG

IF ONLY WE SHTILL HAD THE TORC TO INSHPIRE OUR TROOPSH...

WAIT, I'VE JUSHT HAD A THOUGHT!

POC

?

45

I'M WEARING THE GENERALISSHIMO'J SHEREMONIAL HELMET...

YOU ARE, ILLITERIX?

YESH, DON'T YOU REMEMBER HE GAVE IT TO ME AT GERGOVIA AJ A REWARD FOR MY TREMENDOUSH BRAVERY!

READ MY LIPSH, ILLITERIX! WE'VE GOT A SHYMBOL AFTER ALL, BY BELENUSH!

THERE'J STILL ONE PROBLEM...

PERSHUADING ADRENALIN TO COME TO LONDINIUM WITH USH...

THAT MAY NOT BE NECESSARY, COME AND SEE!

(42A)

WE HAVE TO FACE THE FACTS: OUR LITTLE ADRENALIN'S SPREADING HER WINGS!

WITH ADRENALIN BACK, PEACE AND QUIET ARE RESTORED TO THE VILLAGE...

MINE'S HAD BETTER TRAINING!

FISH UNH

NO, MINE HAS!

UM... ABOUT OUR TRAINING, WE WANTED TO TELL YOU...

THIS ADRENALIN TRIP HAS MADE US, LIKE, THINK ABOUT WHAT WE WANT TO DO...

I'D LIKE TO SEE IF I CAN NAIL BEING A BLACKSMITH...

AND I THINK BEING A FISHMONGER WOULD BE BRILL!

IT WOULD BE GREAT. WE ONLY HAVE TO CROSS THE STREET.

(42B)

SH!

BY JUPITER! IF I'VE GOT THIS RIGHT, THE GIRL AND HER TORC ARE NOW UNDER GAULISH PROTECTION. AS FOR THE TRACKER...

LET'S BE REALISTIC: YOU WON'T BE HAVING AN ADOPTIVE SISTER ANYTIME SOON, MY POOR OLD BRUTUS!

PFF! WELL, I'M NOT MUCH OF A ONE FOR FAMILY...

A FEW DAYS LATER...

I'M CHILLED ABOUT LEAVING, ASTERIX. YOU AND THE VILLAGE ARE WORTHY HEIRS TO MY FATHER!

PEACE IN YOUR HEARTS, BROTHERS, THE GREEN GODDESS BEGONIA WILL WATCH OVER OUR TRAVELS.

BOOHOOOOO, SHE'LL NEVER RUN AWAY AGAIN...

MWAH

YOU'VE BEEN SO GOOD TO ME! WHEREVER I GO, I'LL FOLLOW YOUR EXAMPLE AND HELP ALL CHILDREN IN NEED!

MY SHWEET-HEART!

AND WHAT ABOUT A BOAT FOR YOU?

IT'SH SHORTED! THE FISHMONGER WILL TAKE USH TO LONDINIUM AJ SHOON AJ HIJ BOAT'SH READY!

LET'S GO!

CAN WE HAVE ANOTHER LITTLE TOT...

... TO DROWN OUR SORROWS?

SO ARE WE NOT FOLLOWING HER ANYMORE?

NO, OBELIX, WE'RE NOT FOLLOWING HER ANYMORE.

47

IT IS SAID THAT HER SHIP NEVER REACHED THULE BUT WAS DRIVEN BY THE WINDS TO MORE DISTANT ISLANDS...

HISTORY HAS NOT PRESERVED THE NAME OF VERCINGETORIX'S DAUGHTER...

WAIT! WHERE'S DOPAMIN GONE?

SHE'S RUN OFF AGAIN.

GETAFIX ... DIDN'T ADRENALIN BETRAY VERCINGETORIX'S MEMORY?

NOT REALLY, ASTERIX... NOT REALLY!

BECAUSE HER FATHER TOLD HER TO RESIST CONQUEST AND TO BE FREE, AND THAT'S WHAT SHE DID... IN HER OWN WAY!

44A

AND BECAUJE ALL'J WELL THAT ENDJ WELL AND THERE'J LOTSH OF DELICIOUSH BOAR, EVERY MEMBER OF RAF HAJ BEEN INVITED TO SHARE IN THE GREAT BANQUET...

PAH! THERE ARE PLANJ TO RECONQUER GAUL, DO AWAY WITH ALEJIA AND SHO ON...

...BUT DEEP DOWN ALL THAT REALLY MATTERJ IJ OUR CHILDREN'J HAPPINESSH!

ABSHOLUTELY!

CHOMP CHOMP

THE END

FERRI + CONRAD 2019